Three by Three

Prose Series 18

Anne Dandurand
Claire Dé
Hélène Rioux

Three by Three

Short Stories

*Selected and Translated
by Luise von Flotow*

Guernica

Montreal, 1992

Typesetting by Mégatexte.
Cover Conception by Julia Gualtieri.
Cover Design by Gianni Caccia.

Antonio D'Alfonso, editor.
Guernica Editions Inc.
P.O. Box 633, Station N.D.G.
Montreal (Quebec), Canada H4A 3R1

Legal Deposit — Third Quarter
National Library of Canada and
Bibliothèque nationale du Québec

Canadian Cataloguing in Publication Data
Dandurand, Anne, 1953-
Three by three
(Prose series; 18)
Translated from the French.
ISBN 0-920717-69-1

1. Short stories, Canadian (French) — Translations into English.
2. Canadian fiction (French) — 20th century — Translations in
to English. 3. Canadian fiction (French) — Women authors —
Translations into English.
I. Dé, Claire, 1953-   . II. Rioux, Hélène, 1949-
III. Title. IV. Series.

PS8557.A52T4714 1992 C843'.0108054 C92-090048-8
PQ3919.2.D36T4714 1992.

Contents

Preface

This collection of short stories by three young Quebec authors came about for several reasons. I had been reading and researching contemporary Quebec writing for several years when I first came across their work in obscure journals. It began to surface regularly after a time, and one story even caused a scandal in the Montreal feminist magazine *La Vie en rose,* whose editorial committee could not decide whether it was erotic or pornographic.

I was fascinated by the subjects these writers chose/dared to address, and the eroticism and anger in their texts. For me, the work represented a clearing in the theoretical thicket of feminist writing which had been growing increasingly more dense in Quebec. Their texts focussed on life on the street, in the bars and nightspots of Montreal, and in heterosexual relationships that were never quite perfect. They expressed women's anger and women's fantasies — whether of revenge or erotic encounter — and they were communicative.

This is the aspect I found most enjoyable after reading a decade's worth of cerebral experiments in feminist language and feminist utopias. As far as I was concerned it was time to establish a certain balance in the canon of women's writing in Quebec. Although feminist elements are implicit in the work of these three authors, in their strong women, their assertive use of language, and the angry treatment of the less savoury aspects of 'patriarchy', their work is geared to a wider public. It is accessible, funny in parts, vicious in others, and imaginative. It represents a move away from *l'écriture au féminin* practised by earlier authors, and a move toward narrative.

These stories by Anne Dandurand, Claire Dé and Hélène Rioux are meant as an introduction to a new form of writing developing in Quebec which, though imbued with many feminist sentiments, is pursuing its own course. I have found it great reading, and translating.

Luise von Flotow

Anne Dandurand

Anne Dandurand was born in Montreal in 1953. After work as an actress, a film director and a journalist, she published: *La Louve-Garou* (Short stories, published with Claire Dé, La Pleine Lune, 1988); *Voilà, c'est moi : c'est rien, j'angoisse (Journal imaginaire)* (Short stories, Triptyque, Montreal 1987); *L'Assassin de l'intérieur/ Diable d'espoir* (Short stories, XYZ, 1988); *Un Coeur qui craque (Journal imaginaire)* (Novel, VLB éditeur, 1990); *Petites âmes sous ultimatum* (Short stories, XYZ, 1991).

Dandurand's short stories have been published in numerous literary magazines in Quebec, Ontario, Manitoba and France and have appeared in the following anthologies: *Kanada, Gesellschaft Landeskunde Literatur* (Konigshausen & Neuman, Würzburg, Germany, 1991); *Coincidences*, XYZ, Montreal/ Editions de l'Alei, Dijon, 1990; *Outre ciels*, XYZ, Montreal, 1990; *Nouvelles*, with a prize for young fiction, La Farandole Messidor, Paris, 1990; *Crisis and Creativity in the New Literatures in English*, Rodopi, Amsterdam, Atlanta, 1990; *Les Meilleures Nouvelles de l'Année 89/90*, Syros, Paris, 1990; *En une ville ouverte*, L'Instant même, Québec, L'Atelier du Gué, Paris, 1990; *Celebrating Canadian Women: Prose and Poetry by and about Women*, translation by Luise von Flotow, Fitzhenry and Whiteside, Toronto, 1989; *Ink and Strawberries: An Anthology of Quebec Women's Fiction*, translation by Luise von Flotow, Aya Press, Toronto, 1988; *Invisible Fictions: Contemporary Short Stories from Quebec*, translation by Basil Kingstone, Anansi, Toronto, 1987, *Deathly Delights* (Short stories, Véhicule, 1991), translated by Luise von Flotow.

Photograph of the author by Josée Lambert.

The Theft of
Jacques Braise

Ah, the blond beauty of some men!

I am Jacinthe-Pierre O'Bamsawe, daughter of a Haitian woman and a Cree, forty-five long hard winters old. I am overcome by blond beauty. If not obliterated. This is the story of the error a blond man etched onto my lips: a bane upon his soul.

*

It was an autumn evening, too warm not to tell lies. Three months earlier a cultural magazine had bought one of my erotic drawings for a mean price, and so I was invited to the anniversary of its founding. I decided not to go at first. My real exile begins when I get away from my painting — I much prefer to lose myself in a trompe-l'oeil than in the bottom of a glass — but that evening I was tempted to observe suffering other than my own.

11

Every hermit ends up weakening. The party took place at *Falsification* on Saint-Hubert, you know the bar where, instead of sitting on wooden stools, you sink mercilessly into sinuous leather sofas, white ice floes. The moon punched a hole into the sky, Montreal was reeling under gusts of wind, I set out at three minutes to midnight, the hour of victims and she-wolves.

The place was overflowing with young people under thirty, done up with just enough ostentation to appear marginal, still, the lighting was soft enough for my anti-wrinkle treatment to have effect (a White magic swapped for mauve bills, nothing serious, but where would I be without illusions?). And of course he was there, like July in the gray dullness of November; he was having a feverish discussion with what seemed to be a Venetian prince. A journalist I knew whispered: 'The blond guy, that's Jacques Braise.' My heart leapt; I knew his name from savouring the weekly sweet-sour column he wrote. I manoeuvered to get close to him; I didn't need a drink, I soaked up his blond beauty. Quite by chance, I swear, I picked up three hairs that lay on the back of his black cashmere jacket. I wrapped them in the silver paper of my cigarette pack and put them carefully into my handbag. Then, with my treasure well tucked away, my head was filled with a strange lethargy and I closed my eyes. I had the feeling that I wasn't the one who had acted, but that it was some evil spirit I couldn't resist. I was silent, luxuriating in the moment, and at the end of an hour, Jacques Braise finally turned to me. He seemed delighted to get to know me, he ordered champagne for me, and until dawn he talked to me passionately about his writing. I enjoyed the wine less than the sound of his voice, I was bewitched by his bruise-blue gaze. He gallantly offered to drive me home through almost deserted streets, though not even wild beasts frighten me. A tempest was raging in me, the debacle of all my distress, as though he alone, Jacques Braise, could deliver me from it. And in front of my place, a bane upon his soul, he put his lips on mine, for the duration of one breath.

Some women, perhaps the loneliest, are inflamed by a single fleeting kiss; I am one of those women.

So I tried to see him again. I phoned the magazine several times. The receptionist blocked my calls. I wrote him several times. He didn't reply to my letters. Anyone else would have given up, perhaps wept at the loss of her desire, and returned to her hopeless life, but not me. I am tenacious, dangerous, and mad. Jacques Braise didn't want to give himself to me; too bad, I would steal him.

I found the recipe in my mother's worn book of spells, between the one for ardent water and the one for an elixir against wounds-of-the-past. I began with the first ingredient, and for the first time I was sorry that capital punishment had been abolished. So I watched the local crime column in the *Journal de Montréal* until one Saturday morning I discovered a notice on the suicide of a farmer, Ubald Lusignan, at Saintes-Plaies, a tiny village north of the city. The report explained that the childless widower had hanged himself from the branch of an oak tree in front of his house, because creditors had seized his farm. And so, with a sigh, I got on a bus for Saintes-Plaies. Nothing but work, and hours lost far from my paints. But my lips were on fire; I had to quell the pain.

Soft, dirty snow was falling. In the variety store on the only street in town, the shifty, disagreeable boy with the hatchet face, looked me over for a moment before he showed me the way to Croche road, far out in the country. It was a long walk to Ubald Lusignan's place; on the way I broke the heel of one of my elegant leather boots. The place oozed desolation with its weeds and delapidated shutters. Even the hundred-year-old oak tree implored the heavens. With some difficulty I dug into the hardened soil below the tree, but I found it, and unearthed it. The mandragore, as disquieting as ever in its bleached doll-shape, was almost sniggering. I broke off its left arm, wrapped it carefully in the silvery paper from my cigarette pack and put it with the three hairs. I buried the rest of the root in the same hole. Someone else might need it, you never know, you have to help each other.

It was less complicated to procure the second ingredient. Mama and Papa had often said: 'If you ever need to use us, that's what we are there for.' This was the moment. I crossed the river to the Rive Sud. Below the water, during the gloomy metro ride, I thought about my prey and tried to reason with myself: He is twenty years younger than I am, a handsome boy like that has no interest in an old half-caste woman with shadowy hair and gold teeth, I should leave him to the world of the living. But the nape of my neck and my shoulders were burning, I had no choice but to continue.

The cemetery was frozen over and the moon was on the wane in the silent wind. I went looking for the fifty-year-old dwarf, as pompous as ever in his dark suit, to have him bring the three-meter ladder. As he left, he whispered in his low voice: 'I'll be back in an hour, to close up.' It was a Monday evening; no one would surprise me. Very good.

I perched myself on the top of the ladder in order to reach the uppermost shelf of the columbarium. A shaft of light marked a square constellation just above my head. I opened the small glass door and broke a fingernail. I grasped the large copper imitation book and turned it upside down. From my bag I took a square-head screwdriver and undid the four screws from the base. I removed it. Good evening, Lame Bear

O'Bamsawe, my father of springs and forests. Good evening, Pierre-Josephine Aristide, my mother of flames and fruit. I couldn't prevent myself stroking two fragments of charred bone, one for her and one for him. I thought about my happy childhood when I was rocked to the sound of legends that predated civilization, about gods who could still touch us with their hands. But I didn't spend too much time; I took two pinches of ashes, one from his side, one from hers, and wrapped them in my shiny cigarette paper. Then they too joined the hairs and the root in my bag. I replaced the four screws from the bottom of the funerary urn and put it back in its place. As a thank you, I set an open flask of jasmine oil into the niche, and went off to catch my bus. It would soon be the half hour. I could have taken the ashes of any one of the deceased since nothing is locked away in the mausoleum, but that is not a wise thing to do. There is no better way to be submerged in nightmares.

Although Montreal is nothing but a tainted jungle, it does have certain advantages. To get the third ingredient of my potion, I went to *Onzième Éden*, at the corner of Saint-Grégoire and Papineau, a discothèque for kids under eighteen. It was a Sunday sparking with cold, and the light marked faces and walls. The bouncer, a gorilla with brutal features, didn't want to let me in. I showed him my folder of drawings and explained that I had to make sketches of young people dancing. Sometimes art supplies us with good excuses and convenient rights of passage.

Inside, multicolour spotlights were whirling around, rock music was deafeningly loud, and I took refuge as far away as possible from the loudspeakers. I took out my sketch pad and the pencil with the retractable lead, that makes such a soft fat line. I began drawing, and very quickly had a cluster of girls around me, each one more interested than the other in having herself sketched. I did my best, supplying each one with a portrait; as they posed for me they told me about their lives, their little problems, I listened to them babble on, and lay in wait for my victim. Finally she came along. She was twelve years old 'and a half' she insisted, and had the delicate name Mimosa, which could not have clashed more with her pronounced obesity and her spotty complexion. She seemed ill at ease, and after a lot of hemming and hawing admitted in a whisper that she was having her period. She was afraid she would stain her clothes, and as bad luck would have it, she had no money left to buy another sanitary napkin from the machine. I dropped my pencil and sketch pad and led the girl to the washroom. I put a coin into the distributor and Mimosa took the packet into the seventh cubicle. I took advantage of the moment to correct my eye make-up: the burning was now ravaging my chest, drawing tears from my eyes and making my khol run. I scratched my cornea with the ivory stick. I would like to know why my desires are so irremediable.

Mimosa went off to jiggle about on the dance floor and I slipped into the seventh cubicle. I opened the white metal box, and took out the disgusting napkin covered in good light blood. With the golden scissors inherited from my mother and reserved for witchcraft, I cut out a piece well soaked in blood. I wrapped it in my glistening cigarette paper, and put it away into the little pocket of my handbag. I was nauseated, but some demon, I don't know which one, made me overcome my disgust. The worst was yet to come.

Soon I was unable to sleep as the burning scorched my back right down to my loins. I needed a rat. In Petit-Goave I would only have had to reach down, but in Montreal I had to wait till three in the morning to lift up a manhole cover at the intersection of Saint-Laurent and Rachel. I did it quickly to avoid being spotted by the police. I had tried hard enough to respect the law and get permission to go into the sewers during working hours, but the city workers were aggressive, not cooperative. For three days I wandered from office to office, bumping into closed doors and brusque refusals. As full moon approached, I resigned myself to a change in procedure and a totally illegal operation. I put on my worn leather gear and heavy motorcycle gloves; it reminded me of my Harley-Davidson days when I was twenty. But I forced back my nostalgia, this was not the moment for weakness.

The smell underground was dreadful, but the temperature was warm and welcoming. I turned off my flashlight. The glow from a street light filtered through the grid of the manhole cover. I studied the flow of unspeakable filth, and taking a cube of still bloody filet mignon from my bag, I held it out in my left palm, crouching perfectly motionless on the narrow walkway, at the ready. I thanked my father for having taught me, at the age of about nine, how to catch trout bare-handed in the strong current of the pure Kitchigama river. At that time life was a question of survival, each second had an urgency about it, the future was vague, free of stifling questions and my dreams did not make the days unbearable. I knew how to live then. That's how far I got with my ruminations when I spotted the cunning head emerging from the brownish water. Its eyes shone like jet. I saw it sniff out the piece of meat from a distance. It didn't move, eyeing me scornfully, distrustfully. I stopped breathing. Became as impassive as a mountain. We stayed like that for a century, scrutinizing each other. Finally it slowly swam toward me, scrambled onto the slimy walkway, and edged forward toward my hand. It raised itself up on its hind legs and I could see it was not the youngest, the grey fur on its belly was already quite patchy. It threw itself at the piece of meat like a flash of lightning. Faster still I caught it by the neck. It let out a piercing cry, struggled to get free, but implacably I tightened my hands on its throat. It tried to bite me, ripping at my gloves with frightening incisors. My grip didn't loosen. With a sharp movement, I broke its neck. Afterwards it was child's play to open its jaws and tear out the tongue. I tossed the cadaver into the fetid water, wiped the blood onto the cement, then moistened a gleaming cigarette paper with rat saliva. Finally I had everything I needed.

I returned home as quickly as possible and unwrapped all my shiny papers. With the golden scissors I cut Jacques Braise's three hairs into tiny particles. I added this light dusting to the root of mandragore, the ashes, the virgin's menstrual blood and the rat slaver. Mixed it well with a touch of egg yolk no longer quite fresh, to bind it together. I was furious for not being able to live without obsessions, but I have never had the strength to fight a cyclone and so I ride it out.

When the potion was well reduced after thirteen hours in the slow boiler I caught the precious drop in an Italian ring with a hollow stone, a gift my friend Ada Lazuli brought me from one of her

European tours. It was said to be a Lucretia Borgia ring. I hadn't yet dared to use it, but in war as in war, and in desire as in desire.

The next day around five o'clock I went to wait for Jacques Braise at *Pégase des Ténèbres*, a flashy, noisy bar, next door to the journal offices. I was drinking perrier, craving after him, with the burning in my belly now. My man did not show up. I went again the next day, and the following days. Inexorably, the winter solstice engulfed us a little more each evening. It was a week later that Jacques Braise appeared. My heart tore wide open; how I would have liked life to be different, easier, myself younger, or him older, and a simple love between us. But he ignored me, a bane upon his soul.

He sat at the counter, I edged my way toward him. I offered him a glass of the house beer, a little milky, murky, with a taste of lemon. The bar seemed to conspire with me: a tipsy girl knocked into a waiter who dropped his tray, a customer got angry over the mess on his trousers, another one shouted insults at everyone in general. All this distracted Jacques Braise's attention. I poured the contents of my ring into his beer.

The effect was immediate. He slumped over on me, breaking his glass. I asked the barman to call a taxi before he could get too cold and raise suspicions. Joking about the devastating effects of the house drinks, we laid him on the back seat of the car. It was still snowing so many silent sorrows. The driver helped me carry him to my bed; Jacques Braise was mine, finally. Rather cold for the moment, but that was not important.

I undressed him. His beauty transfixed me; the harmony of his muscular limbs, his torso with the golden mat of hair that would now respond to only my caresses, the sex that would now only protrude for me. I brought a crystal decanter to his tender lips, and pushed its neck into his mouth. His soul slipped into the bottle, a fragile mauve blur. I sealed the stopper with fresh wax and to prevent it from growing cold, I hurriedly buried the essence of Jacques Braise in my cellar, next to the oil furnace. Then I fed the body the antidote, a drink much easier to concoct from a base of salt, perfume and one of my old teeth finely ground (I kept them all, just in case). Jacques Braise returned from the dead, his gaze still a little glassy, and his first action was to embrace me. My theft was a complete success, he was in my power now, my object of adoration, my love zombie.

Of course he can't write his pieces anymore, I dictate them and he signs. At the journal they love his new style. In my painting I now concentrate on truncated perspective.

And at night, when he's resting in my arms, it's unfortunately not with body and soul. But in this *fin de millenium* what more could I have hoped for?

'Le Vol de Jacques Braise' from *Petites âmes sans ultimatum*, XYZ, 1991.

Underground Requiem

I became a murderess after a sudden flash of inspiration. Until then, my life was drab, narrow and useless. And then one night, a call, incomprehensible yet irresistible... An expiation? A vocation? A revelation? I submitted. I withdrew my savings, sold my furniture, ripped up my passport, quit my job, left my house and the few friends I had. I also killed my cat, but he was already very old. Finally, I gave my winter clothes to the homeless: where I was going, I wouldn't need them anymore.

Other women would have entombed themselves in a convent. My particular cloister is less boring than Toronto, less smelly than Paris, and less dangerous than New York. I did not want to return to the open air. I never again wanted to feel cold except in my soul.

I entered my sombre monastery through its nerve centre: the dismal metro station, Berri-UQAM. I had already deposited two suitcases of clean laundry in the lockers of the bus station just above it; everyone has their own itinerary: some people were leaving for Florida or Chibougamau, while I headed down the fibro-cement staircase. In my pockets I carried only a money card and an Opinel knife, signs of my new religion, or of our era.

At the beginning of my noviciate, I took an inventory of the one hundred and fifty kilometers and three million six hundred square meters of tunnels in my underground home; I listed its hundreds of boutiques, doctors' and dentists' offices, hair salons, shoemakers, banks, pharmacies, laundries, restaurants, galleries, its museum, labyrinthine unversity, cinemas, theatres, bookstores, apartment and office blocks, railways stations and the hotels I could reach without breaking my vow; but at the end of one month, in a peach-coloured room at the Chateau Champlain above Bonaventure station, I had a dreadful nightmare: I had become a piece of cheese and felt myself being shredded over a gigantic grater. When I woke up, I understood the message I had been sent: the comfort of this palace was a sacrilege, I had to become a more rigorous ascetic.

I obeyed. In a quiet hour the next day, at Georges-Vanier station, dolled up in a platinum wig, dark glasses and a scarlet mini-dress, I accosted a rather unsavory floor-sweeper, kissed him voraciously and stole his set of keys at the same time; I fled on the next train. From then on I slept in various maintenance lockers, between cleaners' buckets and malodorous tramps. Meditating on this scummy life.

The movement of the crowds gave my day a certain rhythm: in the early hours there were mainly immigrants, their eyes moist with dreams, then students, voluble or taciturn; next a flutter of saleswomen and secretaries wreathed in a thousand perfumes, and then the herd grew sparse, broken old women, a few starchy matrons, some unemployed, arms dangling at their sides, until the harassed five o'clock rush. On theatre evenings I could join the young upper class on the Place des Arts, or I could mix with the jovial, dimwit baseball fans at Pie IX station below their wreck of a stadium, or go rub shoulders with rowdy punks on their way to a heavy-metal concert at the Forum. But it was the emptiness in each of the sixty-five stations at certain precise moments, the nave-like emptiness, that attracted me. Absorbed me. Each station deserted at its own particular hours: a cathedral, a chapel, a sanctuary. I made my eternal vow one Tuesday evening around nine, at Radisson station.

It was between two boat departures, which is what the ticket-takers call the suburban buses loaded up with human cargo. I had gone up to the turnstile level: the moneychanger was nodding off, daydreaming. At the bottom of the stairs that lead to Sherbrooke North, I had contemplated the autumn sky, draped in clouds of mourning. On my right, a lady in a raincoat veered off into the passage leading to the rue du Trianon. Suddenly I heard the stifled sounds of a scuffle. I leapt into a sprint, readying my knife, without knowing why. In a corner displaying an overview of the neighbourhood, the woman was struggling against a man gagging her with one hand. I did not take time to reflect: I crooked my left arm around the rapist's throat, and stuck my Opinel in to the hilt, below his left shoulder blade. The attacker reared up, and let go his prey. I dealt him a few more rapid blows: I wanted to touch his heart. I drew out the blade, turning it to aggravate the injury. The man's struggles grew feeble. Blood began to mottle his black jacket. Horrified, the victim had drawn back. I whispered to her to take off; she did, adjusting her clothes. Leaning against me, the man was in his death throes. He wasn't very tall; his spiky hair was discoloured at the tips. Nasty type... With great interest I watched death shadow his eyes. Afterwards, I carefully laid the corpse onto the blue tile floor, rolled up my soiled cardigan, pushed it under his head and placed his right elbow up over his face. In the next day's newspapers, the lady in the raincoat gave a computer-portrait of her protectoress, but the description of her good Samaritan was the exact opposite of what I am. Already, I was nameless, an anonymous monastic. I remember, I felt divine relief.

A few weeks later, on a Monday, a little before four in the afternoon, I again had to officiate, at Villa Maria Station. The metros had just met up; seven minutes would now pass in silence. Seated on one of the staircases leading to the platforms, I was enjoying the calm before the tempestuous eruptions from nearby colleges. I heard a scurrying sound from the other platform. The footsteps grew fainter, then stopped. Peace flooded over me. Another five minutes of beatitude. My past in the open air became blurred, it seemed to belong to someone else. Perhaps this vocation was inscribed into my destiny well before I was born. Perhaps right from the beginning.

A scream punctured the space. Someone was trying to shove an obese woman onto the tracks. From the pitiful way she was defending herself, it would take less than three and a half minutes to turn her into a bloody mush under the wheels of the first car. I shot forward like a hawk, grasped the guy by the hair and put out his eyes with precise strokes, pushing the knife in just far enough to not touch his brain. One second, the gaze of a maniac, two seconds, streaming eyeballs, four seconds, I was pulling the matron aside, at eleven seconds I was crossing the rails, avoiding the high tension line, and fifty-five seconds later, I was settled in one of the cars, stroking the cheek of a baby asleep in its stroller, and going into ecstasies for its mother over the beauty of innocence.

My ordination took place at Beaudry, the first Sunday of January, well before dawn. (Between November and March I could not stay in recently constructed sections of the metro, because the ventilation shafts bring in a glacial draught that reaches into the very depths of the passages; so I stayed near the city-centre.) Slumped against the two-tone ceramic wall, a dark handsome brute was asleep on one of the benches embedded in brown plastic. I took up a position beside him so that he wouldn't be robbed in his sleep. Doubtless a useless precaution in the aftermath of the holidays when people are recovering, or staying home to escape the polar cold. Implacable, the winter was torturing the country: a puddle of melting snow spread under the man's boots, and the leather was marked by countless crusts of road salt — spilled into the streets at the slightest snowfall. Maybe his expensive leather jacket did not belong to him: the sleeves hung down over his fingers. Did he borrow it? steal it? was it a last-minute gift? A peculiar smell of ether emanated from his seductive body. He woke up suddenly. With a glance he made sure there was nothing to be afraid of. Did he make his confession then because he could sense that eternity lay before me? He revealed all of his miserable existence to me: his tragically curtailed childhood in Pointe-Saint-Charles, his fights, his prison term for bodily injury, the daughter he no longer had the right to visit, his HIV-positive results, and the hellish ritual of coke and crack — he showed me his tortured forearms adorned with rosaries of bruises — his thirty or so tricks a day, and his sole hope of finding the overdose that would send him flying forever. I offered to finish him off with a stab to the heart, a more expeditious and less painful death than the slow agony he was reduced to. He smiled for the first time. Before he accepted, he unbuttoned his shirt. To locate my target, I pressed my ear against his chest where a tattooed swallow was fading away. I sang him an ancient lullaby until, still smiling, he passed away.

Since then, the occasions when I have had to carry out my onerous holy orders have multiplied. Almost everyday now, it just doesn't stop. It makes you wonder whether life above ground...

'Underground Requiem' is the translation of 'Maîtresse des hautes oeuvres', an unpublished text.

Story of Q:
A Dirty Story

I

Perhaps like this: he made her come with his hand and his tongue, until she writhed in apparent pain, then, with him half-resting on the sofa, she would have straddled him backwards and with an implacable rhythm he would have felt himself grow harder still, sucked in and bludgeoned by her sex, until he held her fast by the hips so that the movement could stabilize, accelerate, annihilate him. She would have slumped over on him, sweating, so aromatic, only to rear up again a few seconds later and with her vulva extract a second ejaculation from him. And then a third.

The secret of this chemistry escaped them. He had to go. But before he got dressed, she would have whispered to him: You don't love me, I love you so much I'm kidnapping you. With a syringe she had at hand, she would have pricked him high up on the thigh where the blood still throbbed.

Or perhaps it happened like this: the bar emptied and he had finally doused his thirst. Outside, two women would have stepped up beside him and he would have felt the cold steel of their knives through his leather jacket and jeans. They would have pushed him into the back of a limousine driven by a silhouette, neatly undressed and bound him, and while one of them masturbated him without taking off her glove, the other would have marked his cheek with a long gash murmuring: She didn't ask us to do that, it's for our own pleasure.

II

One way or another, the outcome was the same. He was led into the ballroom of a manor house concealed far beyond the city limits. Through the high French doors, the perfume of lilies of the valley faded like a wave on the icy flagstones.

They didn't allow him to put on his clothes. At the back of the room a strange assemblage of pipes and chains glistened. Doubt. Then apprehension. Don't show that you're trembling.

He was tightly strapped into an iron corset trimmed with rings that fitted between his armpits and his crotch. Steel bracelets were adjusted tightly on his wrists, elbows, knees and ankles. Then he was attached to the scaffold with chains.

With the aid of pulleys he was raised a few inches from the ground, and spread-eagled.

After kissing him on the eyelids, the woman who loved him pulled a leather helmet over his head leaving only his ears and mouth free but covering his eyes.

In a low voice he asked only one question: why the chains?

She replied: To forget.

III

They left him for hours. He heard the leaves rustling in the grounds and, at irregular intervals, men's voices making long moaning sounds in which he could not distinguish suffering from voluptuous pleasure. Sometimes too he heard the whisper of stiff fabric, as though someone were slipping in silently to watch him.

The birds have fallen silent. And his dying mother, his money problems, his uncertain career, his past? After an entire day spent listening, he remembers nothing.

He's hungry. The pulleys move, raising his hands to the level of his chin. He is given a metal bowl, he drinks a thick mixture with a peculiar taste. His head whirls, the situation or the drink?

Never has he felt more alone but he is surprised at how quickly he has forgotten his worries and himself.

Footsteps resonate, a rhythmic clacking, two pairs of wooden sandals? They roll a table up to him, there is a splashing sound of water in a bowl, a glass clinking.

Clear voices softly sing in... Japanese, he doesn't know. The women are laughing. At him?

Four hands massage him. He is groped mercilessly, he blushes under his helmet. Fortunately he no longer is anybody, so what does it matter...

He has a massive erection. The hands are small, almost children's hands.

They flit away. Then his arms and legs his armpits, his nipples, his belly and crotch are wetted. They're soaping him with a shaving brush. They shave him. Everywhere. He's afraid of the blade, an ancient model, but his erection stands.

He's dried off, oiled; he's never felt more naked, more innocent.

Finally the hands touch his sex. They apply a grease with a sugary base scented with opopanax. Indulgent hands slowly move up and down his penis, separating the testicles, holding the gland tight.

Then the Japanese women leave him. The wooden sandals clack like sarcasm.

In the silence his sex burns. The grease! Not only has he lost his identity, he is nothing but an enflamed prick.

IV

No one relieves him. In a corridor of the house a noisy party started up and died down, interspersed by a man's howls.

In the morning a whole cluster of chattering women collects around him. He is placed face down on the ground and his corset removed. He is again suspended by his joints, it is less comfortable this time. A brush touches his shoulder, then his shoulder blade, draws down to between his buttocks.

Laughing, they take him by the limbs. He hears an electric hum, like a dentist's drill.

They tattoo him for hours, he doesn't know exactly. At first the needles are unbearable, but the pain fades by itself. He wants to cry out, but no longer has a voice.

He feels the design, a mythical beast with wings. He would like to know the colours, he doesn't understand why his skin can't read them.

The humming stops. They have finished. They are still all there, pushed up close against him. One mouth touches his tattoo, from bottom to top. He doesn't dare believe it, it's the woman who loves him, he recognizes her kisses. But suddenly a hundred mouths cover him like the belly of an octopus, all these mouths licking him, sucking him, he loses the trace of the one that loves him.

V

He can't take it any longer. He wants to urinate, defecate. He should call but he doesn't dare. He is ashamed. His mask, corset and chains have dematerialized him so quickly. He wants to remain this captive angel. But soon his entrails contort.

He holds back. The first birds welcome the sun. The hinges squeak, someone's coming. They roughly knead his belly and bladder. They masturbate him with unrefined gestures, he couldn't piss if he wanted to now.

They roll up the table, he has the impression that some of them are sniggering. Has he discerned the somewhat bitter fragrance of the woman who loves him?

They work the pulleys, now he is in a horizontal position, like a woman at the gynecologist's, his knees bent and separated. They come closer, he feels their breath against his thighs. Several fingers of varying sizes tease his anus, then they push in a seemingly endless tube. It is a new feeling and in the anonymity of his helmet he smiles with embarrassment and pleasure.

A warm liquid floods into him: how can he absorb so much? His corset fits a little painfully. They nibble at his ears, cover his shoulders with showers of small caresses. Some have taken hold of his sex.

The tube is removed rather too abruptly, he is raised back to a vertical position, his knees pulled up on either side of his waist. They pull a lever. The whole structure supporting him vibrates. He can no longer resist, and lets go all the water in his belly, to the ironic applause of the group.

But he understands that at the same time he is getting rid of everything he reproached himself with in regard to the woman who loves him, his secret cowardice, the half-truths, his escapes... Now, this lightness, this deliverance, this absolution: he promises himself he'll make arrangements to have the same treatment tomorrow.

VI

The tattoo is warming his back. Without releasing him from the irons, they lay him out on the flagstones. A woman sits on his chest. She is naked and her vulva throbs against his chest. Calmly, she opens the lips of her fruit and plunges in the fingers of her other hand. She masturbates slowly on top of him, swaying her rump to her rhythm. Soon she takes two hands to the job, whistling like a cobra, she comes on him, and the exhalations of her orgasm soak his sternum. She has hardly gone when two others settle on his belly and diddle each other. A fourth woman empales herself on the big toe of his left foot. He is assailed by women, by women's sexes all over his body, each one leaving its juice, its moan. Not one of them has wiped him clean, he has the feeling of drowning in all the odours, becoming a bed in a lesbian brothel.

The pulleys hiss, he is raised up horizontally, dripping. He hears dull sounds, of heavy flesh being slapped, he thinks of a muted chant. But no one complains.

They coat him with a warm sticky substance, using a spoon that lingers between his thighs, at his stem. But they continue right up to his mouth. When he sticks out his tongue he can taste. Jam made of apricots and roses? Under his leather helmet he loses control, crickets are shrilling, the sun is leaping like a goat, he founders like a gnat at the heart of a scarlet lady's slipper.

Now they are covering him with a supple dough. A click, and suddenly the temperature increases. They have turned him into a gingerbread man, filled with cream and jam. He waits. He is ready for tea time.

VII

A fountain sobs in the distance. Did he lose consciousness? During the night they laid him on the ground. He kept his mask, but now four large cast iron balls pull at the end of the chains. He is able to move, but only with extreme effort. He must find the woman who loves him, if she is still there.

He opens the rooms, listens for breathing. He realizes he's not the first to wander here: no one wakes up when he leans forward to sniff the bodies.

Dawn is late, the iron scraping on the flagstones makes a moaning sound like sorrow.

What if she is no longer there? For the first time he is really afraid, why this torture if not for her?

Finally he finds her, he says her name, softly, she's sleeping, she doesn't reply. He collapses beside her, drunk on her rather bitter fragrance.

She shudders, sets him free, and says: Go away. He refuses. He says: Leave me my mask and my chains, they are signs of love.

She lies down on him and begins to devour him.

'Histoire de Q' from *Voilà, c'est moi, c'est rien; j'angoisse*, Tryptique, 1989.

Claire Dé

Claire Dé was born in Montreal in 1953, three minutes before Anne Dandurand, her identical twin. After working as a set and costume designer, she wrote many one-act plays for the stage and radio. She was also co-writer with Dandurand of the television detective series *Rachel and Réjean* for Radio-Canada. She has published: *La Louve-Garou* (short stories published with Anne Dandurand), La Pleine lune, 1982; *La Nuit* (art book, lithographs accented by watercolours by Danielle Rochon), Art Global, Montreal, 1987; *Le Désir comme catastrophe naturelle* (short stories, Prix Stendhal, Glénat, Grenoble, 1989), published in Montreal by L'Étincelle, 1989; *Sentimental à l'os* (four plays), VLB éditeur, 1991; *Chiens divers et autres faits écrasés* (short stories), XYZ, 1991. Luise von Flotow has also translated Dé's stories in *Exile Magazine* ('Ce serait la nuit'/ 'It would be night', 1988) and in *Ink and Strawberries: An Anthology of Quebec Women Writers* (Aya Press, 1988).

Photograph of the author by Josée Lambert.

Kill

Today. Wednesday, March 24th. I'm laying into everybody. Five in the morning. The hour of despair. They said so. Yesterday. On TV. That's what came to mind. While I was coming down from our sixth floor apartment. To get croissants. For you. My sweet love. I threw my nutria pelisse on over my underclothes. The building is quiet. Everyone warm under their feather ticks. The neighbour on our landing. A fashionable young man. His parents live on the first floor. Worked on his designs all night. He's an interior designer. Or something of the sort. He showed work at the SAD last fall. The Salon of Artists and Decorators. We were supposed to go. Then I changed my mind. The neighbour. Designs useful things. A serious guy. I know. His office overlooks our bedroom. When I'm not sleeping I watch him. He pulls faces. Sucks on his pencil. His parents must be proud of him.

On the third floor, the august Auguste Dromart. The owner. A Catholic pensioner from Auvergne. Made his fortune with the café. Across the street. Les Cocotiers. A café dressed up in pseudo art deco. Auguste Dromart and Madame go to mass. But not till seven o'clock. The other apartments. Only old women. Paulin. The killer from the 18th arrondissement. He would have had his work cut out for him here. Given the quantity of the merchandise. Old women. Their TVs aren't turned on till about eight thirty. For *Le Magazine de l'objet*. It makes more sense. Getting attached to objects. Than nothing at all. I walk a little way. Still dark. And rainy. A drab day as you'd say in Quebec. Ordinary and boring. But there will be lots of talk around town. I'm about to supply them with a new topic of conversation. I head for the baker on rue Courtalon. The worst one in the neighbourhood. But the only one open at dawn. Her bread tastes like plaster. She renovated. In August. Changed from a dirty little shop into a cream and gold candybox. Trimmed in burgundy. And dirt. But with automatic doors. That's dangerous. Should have warned her.

It gets me every morning. At dawn. The anxiety. Wakes me up suddenly. In a sweat. Pulls me downward. Into blackness. The abyss. Can't even think anymore. Want to cuddle close to. My love. For a semblance of warmth. Or comfort. And you turn your back on me. In your sleep. Like when you're awake. So all I can do is get up. Get dressed. Put on my makeup. Get moving. Read yesterday's *Le Monde*. Anything just to stop crying. Kurds being gassed. Massacres in South Africa. Beatings in Haiti. Torture in Chile. Can't be the news in *Le Monde*. That makes you laugh. The doctor said that's how it is. With us manic-depressives. Cyclical. A period of depression followed by elation. Still. In my case. Elation. Is a long way off.

'Hello, Madame Ficet.'

She's wiping her floor. Barrel-woman. Column-of-Buren-woman. Truncated. Dwarfish. And frizzy. Ever since I've known one like that. A computer engineer. I can't stand that type of bitch. She doesn't move, she jerks. She doesn't speak, she crackles. To make people notice her. From the very height of her insignificance.

51

'What will you have?' Oh, we're in a hurry this morning.

But I'm the only one in the shop! Madame Ficet has got up. Now she's polishing the display cases. With the same dirty rag. She used for the floor. Repulsive. I flash her my loveliest smile. The first one for months.

'Three of your wonderful croissants with pure butter, please.'

She waits on me. With her sausage fingers. That smell of Javex. I pay her. My love. When you get up. I hide in the bathroom. So you won't see me. In this state. My eyes swollen. My hair unkempt. My haggard look. It's a last scrap of pride. It's all I have left. One year. One year today.

'Could you sell me a kilo of bread dough?' I add. 'For my husband. He's having a tarot party tonight. I want to make some mini pizzas.'

'I'll see.'

What exactly does she have to see? I'm over the counter. I'm behind her. She's leaning over her dough box. I push her

52

head into it. The dough goes down with a pleasant plop! Madame Ficet struggles. I hold fast. She's already slowing down. Softening. There we go. Madame Ficet has passed away. Choked on her own dough. Her customers won't miss her. I wipe my hands. On her grimy apron. Grab her keys. Lights out. Turn the *Closed* sign toward the street. Lock the doors. They certainly won't be automatic again. From today.

The morning is graying. Icy implacable damp. I pull up my collar. Put my gloves on. One year today. Not a single day that I didn't try. To ask you for a kiss. A caress. An I love you. Or at least tried to talk about it. With you. My love. Useless.

'It means nothing to me anymore. It's not you.' You always end up saying. 'It'll come back eventually.'

When? When? I wobble on aimlessly. My face turned toward the sky. Let the rain cry in my face. Till I go by the most disgusting shop window in Paris. An exterminator. Twenty-three sewer rats. Stuffed. Since 1925. The twenty-three moth-eaten cadavers crushed in the iron teeth of twenty-three traps. I tried everything. With you. My love.

Everything they recommend. A whole year. In our precious women's magazines. I invested in accessories at first. Net stockings. Sexy lingerie. Pornographic photos. Then I went for theatrics. Pretending indifference. Even taking a fake lover. To provoke in you. My love. A semblance of jealousy. Interest. Finally I gave in to illness. Asthma. Series of bronchitis. Gastric disorders. That brought me a slenderness beyond elegance. No good. Here's the exterminator. Complexion like a winey cockroach. Pig eyes. A faded cap screwed down tight. A grubby shirt tight across his paunch. He's bringing in his daily case of wine.

'May I come in?' I ask.

Whack! A blast of my smile. Seasoned with a batting of the eyelashes and a roll of the shoulder. He's already hot. The rat. He leads the way. Puts his case down behind a table. A bachelor's mess. Smells you prefer not to define.

In public. My love. You are the most delicious of men. Your kindness captures each one of my friends. Who never stop telling me how much they envy me. For succeeding in snagging such a husband. Who works so hard. Got us such a nice apartment. Buys me anything I want. Lavishes gifts on me. Does the dishes. And sometimes even the laundry. You told me. At the beginning. That you were having trouble at work. I believed you. Temporary. It'll pass. That's what I thought. At the beginning.

'What's better? I ask the exterminator. Simpering. Traps or poison? I mean for rats.'

'We even have ultrasound now. Would you like a demonstration?'

I agree enthusiastically. As though there were nothing more interesting in the world. He reaches down under the table. I grab one of his bottles. Smash it down on the back of his neck. Thick, his neck. The bottle breaks. The exterminator submerges into a coma. Into a state well beyond a coma, but what is beyond what? Take a second bottle. Nothing but cheap red. I stave in the back of his skull. With the neck end. Another one dead from drink. The sewer rats will be celebrating.

I leave quietly. Noiselessly. I've been accused often enough of slamming doors. I breathe in the air: carbon monoxyde sharpened with fresh piss. Urine No. 5, the favourite fragance of the *Ville Lumière*. All is well. I turn into the Rue des Halles. Lost in daydreams. Morbid ones. I believed you. It's temporary. It'll pass. That's what I thought. At first. That was before. Before I found out about your mistress. A computer engineer for IBM. Ugly as an oyster's ass. You invited her. To our place. One evening. About ten months ago. To talk shop. You said.

We buy gold, silver and dental debris. They're open. I go in.

'How much for a tooth?'

'All depends.'

He comes closer. A little old man. Bent over, ancient. In a black shiny suit. Beak nose. A few yellowish hairs. Skinny but smooth. I knew immediately. That very instant. That she was your mistress. And that that was the reason. That you didn't. Anymore. Me. It wasn't in your movements. Or your looks. That you and she took great care not to exchange. No. I knew internally. I hated her. On the spot. When I set eyes on her. Everything I have

56

in the way of organs. Heart. Brain. Guts. Knotted up.

'Just yesterday. A sad story. A poor lady. Her husband always invested all their money in his teeth. Only in his gold teeth.'

The old guy's in brilliant form and full of confidences this morning. He adjusts his bow tie. Around his stringy neck. Like a vulture's. Cute.

'She brought me all of them. Thirty two. Kind of crazy. But who isn't, right?'

'Right.'

I talked to you about it. Asked you straight out. If she was your mistress. You swore to God she wasn't. I was crazy. I was making a mistake. How could I! But don't you trust me? You exclaimed. I did trust you. I believed you. But you kept on. Not to. Me. I half-open my coat. The old guy steals a glance. That gets stuck on my half-bra of mocha lace. Then slips to the skin of my breast. Fragile. Trembling. He continues. A little temptation.

'When he died she got it all back. Thirty two gold teeth of excellent quality. I gave her a good price.'

'That's interesting. Will you show me?'

He doesn't refuse. Opens a drawer. A revolver. Next to a blue velvet case. He takes the case. I take the revolver. I rub up against him. Get it up one last time, grandpa. I think about that poor woman. Who endured her husband's craziness. So many years. I imagine her. Pulling the corpse's teeth. With a pair of plyers. Whatever the price. The old guy gave her. It will never be enough. Never. I pull the trigger. At the same time. Farther off. A car alarm goes off. No one heard me. Thanks for the people who steal car radios. The pawnbroker's jaw lands between my breasts. He died happy. With an erection. I pocket the revolver. Maybe I can use it. You shouldn't be allowed to buy firearms. It increases the crime rate.

It's stopped raining. But there's still the damp. Getting into me. Chilling me from inside. I have the feeling I'm about to go crazy. Crack. And crumble like the rocks in the country I come from. I suddenly realize. The croissants are still there under my arm. I need some fresh milk. A few steps to the right. Then to the left. A couple of lap-dogs are taking their lethargic owners for walks on leashes. The Arab is there behind his counter. A nice podgy Arab. With the watery eyes of a spaniel. He's cleaning his nails. With his Opinel.

'How are things?'

'Better all the time.'

Two months ago. You lost your keys. You said. Actually, she stole them. So. Three days later. You got a call. From her. I know. I'm the one who answered. You made me a sign. To go away. It's about work, OK. That's what you said. A couple of times that evening you muttered she's the one who wants it this way. She's the one who wants it. An ultimatum from her. Probably. Along the lines You leave her or I leave you. And like all men. You're a coward. Want your extra-marital fluff alongside your domestic houseplant. So your affair. Was cut short by your mistress. But. Even afterwards. You continued. Not to. Me.

At the Arab's. I take my three liters of milk. What I need for twenty four hours. I pay. He lets go of his Opinel to make change. I insert the knife under his ribs. Push upward with a cool stroke. Blood gushes from his mouth. I must have touched a lung. He opens his eyes wide in surprise. More like a spaniel than ever. Almost touching. Leans forward toward me.

'Did you know? I tell him. A scientist in Texas. Found that excessive consumption of milk. Can aggravate homicidal tendencies. They all wrote him off as a fool.'

Until you asked me. Another evening. To find you some files. In your desk. It fell out. Out of the stack of files. An envelope. Opened. With two letters. In your handwriting. Your handwriting. The Arab collapses on his till. I pull the Opinel out. Not that much blood. Maybe that's what an internal haemorrhage is like. I hope it won't be peddled as a racist crime. For me it's not the Arab, it's humanity in general. Myself in particular and in first place. I go out and forget my milk. And my croissants. Doesn't matter. I don't like those croissants anyway. Too soft.

Then I finish off a tramp. Relieve him of himself. He was sleeping it off. Huddled up on the ground in front of a Portuguese restaurant. With a couple of blows of a steel bar. Lying close by. Building material left around. Endless roadworks. Streets constantly rebuilt. Which doesn't help the traffic. Or the parking. And there's one of those fiends in baby blue. Her Bic pen erect, well into her book of tickets, a meter maid off to war already. So early in the morning! She's getting ready to stick a ticket. On my sweetheart's BX. At this time of the morning! I run at her. Push her into an entrance.

'It's not bothering anybody there!'

'Madame...'

She didn't have time to finish. I took her off guard. I pulled her white scarf down around her neck. The baby blue meter maid doesn't know anything anymore. Or what to do. With a woman attacking her. It's usually men. Usually. In the first letter. You were complaining. To her. The engineer from IBM. In a first letter. About her indifference. That it was hard for both of you. I'll manage to impose your presence on my wife. Is what you wrote. It's practical. You added. She will take care of the shopping, the housekeeping and the cooking. And she's a good cook. That too. You had to spoil that for me. Deprive me of it. The pleasure of cooking for you. The baby blue meter maid. Tied a white scarf over her cap. To protect it from the rain. The cap that matches her baby blue uniform. She must think she's Sylvia the stewardess. Maybe that makes up for the insults she hears all day long. Poor thing. In the second letter you complain too. About her moving from a friendly complicitous relationship. To outright hostility. We're finished you wrote. Finished with snuggling on the sofa together for a cuddle. Finished with visiting, talking, cuddling and dreaming. And how much you regretted it. While I. For a whole year. She's the one. Who must have hidden the letters. In your files. She knew. That I would end up reading them. Sooner or later.

I pull tight. Twist the white scarf. Under the baby blue chin. She struggles harder. Than Madame Ficet, the late baker. Scratches my face. Tears a piece out of my fur pelisse. I don't let go. Baby blue meter maids are something unnatural. My sweet love won't catch it. Not today. Still. I wonder whether he would have paid it. The ticket. With the presidential elections in a few months. They expect a presidential amnesty. They make gestures like that. I will never know. If it helped.

The streets are getting busier. I run across greasy slippery paving stones in my stiletto heels. Almost fall a couple of times. Put a run in one of my black stockings. Cross the Rue de Rivoli slipping between cars. Outburst of honking. Come out on the rue Bertin Poiré. Then at the Codec supermarket. And the owner of the Codec. As bellipotent as he is omnipotent. A little dictator in a large expanse. I put on a woeful face.

'Monsieur! Monsieur! '

He puffs himself up. Turns himself into the man-who-understands. Into the strong-man-who-protects-the-weak-little-lady-in- distress. I go in with him. Then throw myself into his arms. Sob to break his heart. It's easy, my nerves are raw. He pats me on the back and repeats Come on now, come on now little lady. If there is one thing I detest it's being treated as a little lady. Those two letters. To think I knew everything. From the start. Idiot. It's even worse. Having known. And denied it. In order to discover it later. What I already knew. And was trying to ignore with all my strength. You lose all confidence. Confidence in others. In you. In myself. Especially in myself. Generalised filth. Spread over our finest memories. The past. The future. Every mouthful of life. Difficult to swallow. Because of the taste. Of everything. A disgusting taste. When you blame it on work. On work or anything else. How can I believe you now? How can I believe anything? Bang! The fat-bellied Codec despot collapses. His tyranny over the Vietnamese cashiers is herewith over. You make the revolution you can. Only one regret. I haven't got time to bury him. Under a mountain of deep-frozen food.

It's almost light now. Changed from anthracite gray to lead gray. I lean against the wall of the *Flor Rivoli Hotel.* Two fading stars. Catch my breath. When I look up. A policeman is coming toward me. With my coat open over my underclothes. The run in my black stockings. He thinks I'm a whore. He's in the new uniform. By Balmain. The American look, is what they all say. And they like it. It looks more serious. Not to me. They all look like security guards. I preferred the képi. More typical.

'Papers, please.'

I seize the cop's fingers. Shove them in between my thighs. His jaw drops in sudden amazement. He's really young. Straight out of Police School. Pimples and all. I force open his lips. With the barrel of my revolver. Bang-again! It spurts. But not as nicely as with Alain Delon. In *Three Men to Kill.* In that one it sprayed across a mirror. A dazzling red. Here it's his acne-covered face. His gelatinous brain. Everything. That splatters me. That's the pain. At the movies. Death is always prettier. Like things on TV. It all gets too pretty. Now, let's hope that. His friends from the cop shop. Let's hope they don't take too long. And don't hesitate to use their guns. If I have to, I'll kill some more. Anyone within my reach. So the cops will use. Their guns. On me. Forgive me my love. You won't have your croissants this morning. Or your tarot party. Auguste Dromart, the august owner. Or the neighbour on our landing. Or one of the old women in the building. Someone will let you know. Or a colleague. Or one of your friends will phone. Or you'll read about it yourself. In tomorrow's society column in *Le Monde*. A crazed woman executes a number of people in the first arrondissement. I couldn't resign myself. To you no longer touching me. No longer making love to me. I couldn't resign myself. To leaving you. To killing you. Or to killing myself. Desperate. From always hoping. From still hoping. Every moment. That you love me, love me, love me. Suffering. Every moment too. Realizing that no. You don't love me anymore. While in order to continue living I would have had to. Give up all hope.

'À tuer' from *Le Désir comme catastrophe naturelle*, published by Glénat, 1989 and l'Étincelle, 1990.

Lipstick

The weather is cool, the sky lowering and this morning, like every morning before she goes out, the woman paints her lips bright red, blood red. The weather is cool, the sky lowering and this morning, a twenty-second of January, a sudden fear, fear in this lipstick, a diffuse fear that all other mornings will be the same as this twenty-second of January — a monotonous string of the twenty-second days of January, without relief, all identical until the last — the woman would paint her lips red before going out as though nothing were wrong, while the fear would grind her head and her body making her tremble, the fear that her heart was no longer beating since her lover left her. And so this morning the woman applies her lipstick like you build a wall, like you put on armour, for nothing, a derisory but elaborated gesture, the woman paints her lips but only sees her lover's mouth, his mouth endlessly, as she would gorge herself on his voice, his hands, his skin, his sex — but this morning nothing — nothing except the lowering sky, I'm cold, and nothing except this lipstick, a wall, a derisory armour, the woman feels her senses and her spirit affected and changed — she knows nothing anymore, this woman, she can no longer say ah! yes, kiss me again, love me, think about me sometimes, the weather is cool, my memory in shreds, your body in pieces, space, weather, desire crushed, atomized, absence, this evil, these crumbs. My life lipstick.

'Baton de rouge' from *Le Désir comme catastrophe naturelle*
published by L'Étincelle, 1989, 1990.

Once upon a Time

Once upon a time. Summer, a Sunday in late July, in a suburban garden with a hedge of almost perfectly green poplars at its border, a sky of almost immutable blue, and a moist breeze, all creating an illusion of countryside, during a dinner with friends, under an arbour of wild bryony, around a massive granite table, couples that see each other because the husbands share business interests, while the wives exchange remarks on their secular heritage, children, illnesses, food. But one of the women hardly eats, hardly speaks, and we know from her accent that she is a stranger. With her usually lowered eyes, her bare shoulders, her dark hair gathered in a chignon under a white silk chrysanthemum, her delicate neck thus revealed, her bowed nape, she is like a slender plant, fading, declining. Then she leans her head on her lover's shoulder, raises her eyes to him, black eyes, somber pools at the bottom of a well and that is exactly how she feels, at the bottom of a well. Up there lies life, life's noises, fragments of conversations, murmurings, inaudible, inaccessible, and this is where her love has taken her, to the bottom of a well, while beyond the well they torture, they South-Africanize, they starve, and her own country still colonized, uncertain, torn, and that's all she sees, this stranger, the tearing between people. But she knows how unimportant her own tearing is, she knows how ridiculous, how petty it is, but the tearing is still there, the gash, the break, the stranger closes her eyes again, this is not the moment, it is never the moment, the hostess says Come on, we're among friends. The stranger drinks a little of the muscadet waiting in her glass, while her lover rests his elbows on the table and leaves her his shoulder. He smokes a cigarillo, discusses profit margins, savours an armagnac, while she with her black eyes fixed on his neck, they're growing darker again, and her heart beats a little faster, a little stronger, as it does each time she looks at her lover for awhile, but someone is taking a photograph of the dinner guests, asking the stranger to stand up, asking her to smile. One last smile before my suicide, says the stranger, everyone laughs. Why are you talking like that? her lover asks. Because, and she says nothing more than this Because, because he betrayed her, because he lied to her for months and months, because she is angry with him, because she is even more angry with herself, yesterday for believing him when he lied, today for still loving him. But her scattered friends, her sister, and total strangers, other women she met on buses or in bars, all of them, advised her to leave him, the oldest among them even said You'll see, one day, you'll end up praying, praying not to love him anymore. But you don't pray at the bottom of a well.

Once upon a time. Summer, a Sunday in late July, in the garden of a middle-class home, during a dinner with friends, with muscadet, armagnac, Come on, this is not the moment, it is never the moment, that's when her lover turned toward her, that's when he would have seen her black darkening eyes, he would have kissed her, there at the nape of her neck, while she would have said in his ear Come on, follow me. She would have left the table, entered the house and in the semi-darkness would have climbed right up to the attic, to a little storage room with an old mattress, cardboard boxes, shadows and dust, he would have joined her there, found her there, leaning against a wall, her hair undone, the white silk chrysanthemum on the floor, holding her dress in one hand, biting her arm. He would have drawn close, his whole body against hers, his weight on her, she seeking his tongue, drinking it in, her dress has fallen, she presses close, holds him as if she wanted to anchor herself to him, as if at the edge of a storm. Her mouth still on his, her hands on his belly, between his legs, she grasps him, their lips part, so much sweetness palpitating between her palms, moving her, but two of his fingers are already digging into her, gouging her again and again, into her pleasure. Then he thrusts into her, grinds her, files her, grates her, gashes her, splays her. Sweat, sobs. And spasms.

Once upon a time. Summer, a Sunday in late July, in a middle-class home, after a dinner with friends, muscadet, armagnac. Come on this is not the moment, she would have gone up to the attic, into the small storage room where shadows are spreading. Afterwards it was the woman who drew away from him, curled up at his feet, embraced his leg, raised her face to that point, the man leaning back, wanting and not wanting, letting himself go, and for a long time they stayed like that, the woman's face in the man's briny moisture, when he burst into her throat and moaned Oh yes, I love you. Then she told him Go away, leave me alone. And he went away to join the others while she cried, wishing she were filled, flooded, overflowing with him. It is all too much for her, it gags her, imprisons her and she doesn't even try to escape. So she joined the others, and he, her lover, guessed she wanted to leave as quickly as possible. They thanked the hostess, and in the fast lane, she asked him to caress her, his one hand was on the wheel, with the other he made her come.

Once upon a time. Summer, a Sunday in late July, in a middle-class home, after a dinner with friends, muscadet, armagnac, Come on, this is not the moment, she would have gone up to the attic, into the little storage room, shadows and dust, where he did not come to join her, and afterward in the car after he'd made her come, she put her head on her lover's shoulder, thinking

73

not without displeasure, that this was the only thing that counted for her. Sex, her religion. Her passion, a poison. Loving, a crime. Love, her only fairy tale.

'Il était une fois' from *Le Désir comme catastrophe naturelle*, published by Glénat, 1989, and l'Étincelle, 1989.

Hélène Rioux

Hélène Rioux was born in Montreal in 1949, and began writing early. After producing largely poetry during her childhood and adolescence, she turned to prose and published a first collection of short stories, *L'Homme de Hong Kong*, in 1986. The short story by the same name won her a prize in the Radio-Canada short story competition. She has published also collections of poetry, *récits*, and two novels, the most recent being *Les Miroirs d'Éléonore* in 1990 (a finalist for the Governor General's Award). She has collaborated in numerous reviews and journals in Quebec, has translated extensively from English, and is on the editorial board of *XYZ*, the journal specializing in short stories. She has published: *Les miroirs d'Éléonore*, Lacombe, 1990; *L'Homme de Hong Kong*, Québec/Amérique, 1986; *Une Histoire gitane*, Québec/Amérique, 1982; *J'Elle*, Stanké, 1979; *Un sens à ma vie*, Les Éditions La Presse, 1975; *Yes, monsieur*, Les Éditions La Presse, 1973; *Suite pour un visage*, Carré Saint-Louis, 1970.

Photograph of the author by Kèro.

The Man from Hong Kong

He was born in Hong Kong, pushed out into the enormous city, a city of multitudes. He was a child in the streets of Hong Kong, amid the torrid crowds. He grew up in its slums, breathing in the foul exhalations of its alleys. As an adolescent he explored the skyscrapers, bewitched by the mirrors, the neon lights, and the asphalt. He stole to play the slot machines, the video games, in the noise. There, listening to loud music, in rooms saturated with strident cries he dreamt of America. Until very late at night, very loud. That was long ago. He was twenty-four now.

It was in Hong Kong that he first read the true story in the papers, the story of Charles Manson, whose angry face, splashed across the first page he gazed at and fixed in his memory. That happened in America, in California, the Eldorado. There had been a lot of blood, blood everywhere, on the walls of the houses, and in the gardens, among the flowers. As a young child he liked blood, its colour, its sweetish smell. He liked roaming around the abatoirs, listening to the sounds of the animals going to slaughter.

He had been walking for weeks, propelled by the strongest instinct of all, he walked without a break, he was in hiding. He had become public enemy number one. He had a nickname, when they talked about him, they said 'the man from Hong Kong', as though there were only one. He'd escaped into the woods, eating wild fruits, young shoots, anything. His clothing, stiff with grime, had given out at the seams. He was dirty and alone.

Being alone was new, they were two before, there was Gary before, his accomplice, like a brother in pleasure. Gary was dead. And all the others too, the victims. The smell of blood stayed in his memory. And the cries, long and slow. All sorts of cries. Moans, rattles, gurgles, howls. All sorts of expressions. Hate, terror, desperation, madness, depths of despair. All sorts of emotions. Mirrors. Sometimes, deep down, there was a spark, something beseeching.

He had crossed the United States from south to north on foot. He was a hare in the woods, a rat in the fields, a scorpion in the desert, a part of the landscape, camouflaged in the dunes, running, crawling, always fleeing. He walked along the shore. He avoided the villages. He knew his photo was on the first page of all the newspapers. He was the most wanted man on the American continent, public enemy number one. He was often hungry. That's when he thought about Hong Kong, his home town. He would tell himself he was walking to Hong Kong, and that one day as part of the crowd, he would be forgotten. Or he'd hide on one of the islands. He thought about the islands and the silent junks that slipped across the choppy water. At the heart of the acrid stench, when his guts were screaming starvation, his thoughts were his nourishment.

They were hunting him down, the pack following his trail. Gary foresaw the end and wore a ring filled with cyanide, like the commandos in the war. He swallowed the poison in his cell, after they caught him, and died quickly without confessing anything. But he didn't have a ring on his finger. Only a single line crossed his bare hands, the life line, right down the centre. He had to save his life, and that was why he was fleeing along deserted roads and sleeping in ravines.

For several days he had walked along the wild shore of the Pacific. He opened mussels, ate them raw and full of sand that he spit out again. He drank salt water. Most of the time he thought about Hong Kong, or he thought about nothing at all. At night he slept, rolled up tight. He slept like a cat, always on the alert.

It was in Hong Kong as a young boy that he had learnt martial arts. He dreamt of being a ninja, a black angel. Legends haunted his memory. Later he taught karate in San Francisco, that was how he met Gary, teaching him karate. He knew how to kill, a single finger into the solar plexus. But he had killed his own victims slowly.

He had had a lot of victims. The newspapers said about thirty. The police based their guess on the number of people gone missing in California in a year, and on the bones they found in the cellar besides the corpses. And on the people in the films that he and Gary made. The police found the camera and a few rolls of film. They didn't know the exact number. Nor did he, he didn't know how many people he had tortured in his cellar.

The first time he had to flee was from Hong Kong, after he raped the little girl. He'd had to flee. He went to Macao by ship. Then to Bangkok and Singapore.

He had liked the way the little girl's suffering was true, and the way her death was real. He'd liked this truth.

He had picked her up in a park, a quiet child surrounded by her toys, a shy child that hadn't learnt to say no to adults. There had been blood when he raped her, blood had stained his hands, his clothes, his genitals. The same blood spread out over the clumps of yellow grass, the stunted bushes. She was a very small child, very young, maybe four years old, her eyes open wide upon her fear and a grimace when she cried. He raped her in an empty lot, so he could hear her cries. He had liked the way her cries were real. And the terror in her gaze, he had liked that. He had killed her slowly.

That wasn't the first time he killed. As a child he'd torn the wings off dragonflies. Later he hanged puppies and drowned cats. The cats, he had drowned slowly.

Down there on the lonely farm in California, he had had a dog, a frightening mastiff with a foaming muzzle, a monster. He reserved it for the victims. The people who bought his films had particularly liked that. First the scene where the man had to confront the dog. The woman, meanwhile, was tied up. In the film you saw a close-up of her face. She was terror-stricken, crying. He remembered this appalled look, the tears.

He had trained the dog himself, hard. He turned him into a pitiless killer, a fierce, relentless killer. The child was also tied up. A little boy. Crying. The mother was ready to do anything to save him, as the dog tore apart her husband who was hopelessly trying to protect his eyes and his genitals. His customers were wild about the scenes of animal love. To make these scenes more convincing, he made her believe her compliance would save the child. Afterwards, there wasn't much left of her. A heap of shredded flesh, a prostrate shape that barely moaned. He had left her to the dog. The child too. He knew no pity. His clients had paid a fortune for that film.

He had been walking for weeks, and for weeks he had been hungry. All the money from the film sales was in the bank, he couldn't withdraw it. The money from his victims' wallets, too. He thought about this money and about his hunger. He ate algae. He washed in the sea. He washed for a long time. He jumped with the waves. When they passed over his head, he let himself be carried and thrown onto the beach. He laughed. He was alone, laughing, a loud, full-throated laugh. The thunder of the ocean covered over his laughter. He was not afraid of drowning. He confronted these high forceful waves that roared as they fell upon him, she-lions of the sea.

In Hong Kong he lived a few months with a Chinese girl, a bloodless girl who didn't speak much, but laughed about everything in the bars almost solid with smoke. At night, in the room, standing in the frame of the bathroom door, her head tipped back, she would laugh, her hair undone, and hanging down to the floor. Her skinny body, when she was naked, she laughed at her scrawniness. When she ate, it was always rice she ate quickly with her fingers, in small balls. When she made the vein in her arm stand out and pierced it with the syringe, she was still laughing, then she would close her eyes. It was in Hong Kong and he was sixteen in the city night. Sometimes he thought about this girl whose name he'd forgotten, and about the room that was so dirty, and about her asleep on the floor in the garbage. He hadn't hurt this Chinese girl because of the laugh, and the empty eyes. He didn't want the laugh to stop, there was an equilibrium in this immense laugh. He particularly liked the endless emptiness, her eyes after the heroin injection, just before she closed them and fell asleep.

The sun was going down, soon it would be lost in the ocean. For weeks he had been walking north, toward the point where the sun never sets at the edge of the horizon. One night he crossed the border, he was in Canada, he was walking in this country and the landscape didn't change. He thought about the ships that leave the port of Vancouver for Asia, and he thought that maybe he could make the trip, hidden in a hold, among sacks of wheat.

In Canada his photo had also appeared in the papers. They were talking about the 'man from Hong Kong', the sadist, the crazy. Like some vile and dangerous beast, the same way they'd talked about Charles Manson. They described the tortures he had invented in detail. The readers shuddered, as they read the descriptions. The people who bought his films had shuddered too. The truth of those shattered faces, twisted mouths, had fascinated them. Torture used to be carried out in public and crowds would collect to see the spectacle, grab the best spots on the platform around the gibbet, warm themselves at the pyre. Gladiators fought wild animals in the arena. The condemned were brought in carts, then pushed to the scaffold in the midst of hooting and laughter. Pedlars circulated, selling tasty snacks the spectators could relish through the agonies. Obscene winks punctuated the rush of a vast collective delirium of flesh. When everything was over, couples would hurry away to their alcoves. Oh! the wild orgasm, the paroxysm of pleasure. He closed his eyes, violently. He knew he would have been the best of the exe-cutioners. In another time, somewhere, he had doubtless been one. He still had a confused throbbing memory of it. He would have brought death on slowly. He knew all the refinements, all the subtleties and tricks. He knew how to play with it, calling it forth then letting it wait, bringing it on again, for hours. Death, an insatiable lover.

He thought he had acted without hatred, he said it aloud to the sea, no, it wasn't hatred that guided his hands. It was like the ocean when it is unleashed, it was like the swirls that come from the depths where, since the night of time, beasts deprived of light have evolved. One day he had finished a painting he called Atlantis in which he tried to reproduce this ancient hideousness, crushed under tons of salty water, warts, tentacles, blisters, in the splendour of a lost continent.

No, he had felt no particular hatred toward the people he held in chains in the cellar of his farmhouse, they were taken by chance, like animals that wander into a trap. But he had loved their deaths, he had wanted them long and slow; you could say it was in their death that he had loved them, when the last breath of life left in them wanted the *coup de grâce*. He would lean over them and seek the moment when the eyes suddenly glaze over, when the struggle ceases, the muscles and nerves finally relax, this micro-second of eternity, one of the most privileged moments, a mysterious rebirth.

It was true that it had amused him to invent strange tortures. He consulted archives, built instruments. He knew how to find the vulnerable spots, the most sensitive places, the secret zones. He also liked to force his prisoners to all kinds of base acts, ridiculous postures. He said he was unveiling their hidden lusts, revealing them to them. He liked making films of suffering; yes, when he pushed them into the cellar and they finally understood what they could expect, the terror that gripped them, made them stiffen or fall to their knees. He loved the resistance and the loss of dignity. Some would call upon their gods who no longer responded. Others turned into grotesque figures when they faced death. Convulsions and grimaces while he laughed.

He kept statistics, made bets with Gary about how long they would last. Their endurance sometimes amazed them. The body's resistance, the will to continue living, even mutilated or debased. As long as there was hope. He knew how to make the hope last a long time, and he always won the bets. The money wasn't really important since they shared it. Sometimes they would only bet a pack of cigarettes, a beer, or the price of a table dancer at the strip bar of the motel. It was just fun, the pleasure of the game.

He stopped walking. The nausea wouldn't leave him anymore. His own smell, raw mussels, seaweed, sweat. The night before he had ventured into a small town, a peaceful little place with gardens behind the houses. He didn't steal any vegetables, but he ransacked the garbage cans of the restaurants, and picked up the cigarette butts in the street. He was ashamed of these furtive gestures of poverty. As a child in Hong Kong, he picked up squashed fruit that fell from the shelves.

A sound of footsteps gave him a sudden start. A woman walked by, her hair tossed back, her heels clicking on the sidewalk. He could have grabbed her by her hair, twisted it, knocked her down and broken her head on the asphalt with one blow. Just to satisfy the savage instinct that was lodged in him. The image surged up, dazzling, and blood rushed to his head. He had the impression his brain was swelling, touching the sides of his skull, and his skull was about to burst under the pressure. He clenched his fists in his pockets, his hands were trembling. The woman passed in front of him, she seemed to be walking in a rage, her heels clacking, she passed without a glance.

He could have followed her — he had been walking alone for such a long time, only to put distance between his judges and himself, he could have walked further to kill this woman he didn't know in the peaceful night. As she walked by he saw she had the hard kind of beauty you associate with amazons or courtesans. He had hesitated. The trembling in his hands transferred to his whole body.

The trembling, the pressure in his skull, it was Hong Kong collapsing in an avalanche. A nightmare. It was enough for one woman to walk by without a glance and she annihilated Hong Kong. The stones of Hong Kong fell in a thunderous noise, he would never be able to return to Hong Kong. Or to the silent junks tacking between the islands. His endless walk made no sense. Hong Kong no longer existed.

For a long time he heard her heels on the sidewalk. He was alone in the light of the streetlamp. Then he went down to the sea. At dawn he was there. He stood motionless, looking at the town sinking into the Pacific.

Now the sun was definitely swallowed up. They said that far in the north, it never set. But he felt like diving into the waves, letting himself be drawn to the bottom to join the mysterious beasts that live without light.

Perhaps, Atlantis.

'L'Homme de Hong Kong'
from *L'Homme de Hong Kong,*
published by Québec/Amérique, 1986.

Sisyphus

At first there is a man pacing in his apartment. It is evening. The man is alone. He is talking to himself about the play he wants to write and imagining the production. Then there is the telephone ringing off the hook. And he doesn't answer. There is music, Prokofieff.

There is his slow voice, punctuated by silences.

This is what he has done all his life. He has walked back and forth, imagining books to write, productions. Journeys.

His hair is gray, rather long at the nape. He has a slim body. His clothes are elegant yet casual.

'The music, to start with,' he says. '*Romeo and Juliet*. Total darkness. The set will appear bit by bit, bathed in an uncertain, diffuse light. An unimaginable set, something completely surrealist. Outlandish.

Colourless. Leaden, slate, fog. No man's land... I really like this inhuman image.'

His voice is solemn, smooth. His diction, impeccable, even affected, you could say.

'Someone steps forward, dressed in red, wearing an ample, very long robe. The hair is surprisingly motionless. It is a woman, but this is conjecture before it is certain. Scarlet, splendid... The man comes forth from behind a rock on the opposite side of the stage. Dressed in royal blue. Yes, that's it. She is ablaze, while he... impenetrable, ruthless. They meet without faltering. They are blind. Their fixed gazes almost demented. They move away from each other. Then there is a loud cry, from far away and nearby. From everywhere. Indefinable. A cry that seems to hold all the wretchedness in the world. Silence, then the woman speaks.'

He stops walking to pour himself a drink. For a long time he watches the golden liquid shimmer in his glass. He thinks. He thinks the woman could be pregnant, about to give birth.

'Yes, that's beautiful,' he says. 'I very much like the idea of childbirth. With the ample red robe, yes, that's exactly it, very suggestive... They continue walking. Following parallel paths. No meeting is yet possible, even foreseeable. And the cry, the cry is immense. Perturbing, it tears the eardrums. The movements are slow, invisible chains hamper the characters' gestures. She stretches her arm into emptiness, she clasps nothingness.'

He stops again. All his life he has done nothing but walk back and forth, stop and start again. He thinks one day something brilliant will come out of him, and confound the universe.

'He looks at her,' he says. 'I know, she's the one who is blind. He sees her and observes her very soul. She is defenseless. He notes how vulnerable she is despite all this red she displays like a banner. Arrogant and defenseless. He talks to her, not unpleasantly, he's even gentle. She casts a desperately expressionless gaze about her.'

'There should be an inkling of a closed door in a corner of the set, a closed door that blocks them like distraught insects at night. No, I'm getting off track. That's not it, no, it's unreal, the place is timeless, all the action must be located beyond time and space... Although a door, in this landscape of stone and mist, is an unexpected element I shouldn't completely forget.'

Again the phone rings, he prefers not to answer.

'Occasionally a metallic sound would come into the music,' he says, 'a creaking, a moving of chains from the *oubliettes*. This noise would seem to be filtering through centuries-old walls. The gestures would become heavier and less free.'

(I haven't told you that during working hours this man sorts letters at the Ministry of Communications where his colleagues derisively nickname him the Poet because of the white silk scarf he wears over his turtle-necks, the gray curls at his nape, and his rather grandiose, bombastic vocabulary. I haven't told you either that in the early evening he frequents trendy bars where thanks to the same scarf, the curls and the vocabulary, he manages to seduce very young women whom he accompanies to their homes, striding through the rain, and whom he kisses chastely on the forehead before taking his leave. Then he invites them to small intimate suppers during which he calls them 'my muse' and recites Baudelaire or Lautréamont; in his conversation he drops the names of painters and philosophers, who he says have been misunderstood, and his comments are adorned with quotations. He always sheds a few tears at the end of these suppers, his head in his hands, saying, 'What's happening to me? What's happening to me?' He never fails to emphasize the girls' beauty and talk about the dresses he wants to have made for them by one of his designer friends, or about the holidays they could spend together at the seaside, the exotic cities they could visit, Shanghai or Singapore, or Beirut where they would hear the Tetralogy, or Florence where they would stroll on the Ponte Vecchio, and the countless splendours — it is true that for the adolescents he seduces, this man's culture seems to have no bounds; and then he talks about the great work he wants to write, he will write, and about the fact that just resting his hand on the girl's knee on a cafe-terrace makes him ejaculate, and when that happens he says he has never before been so ardently in love. But after a few weeks of what he calls their preliminaries, he wants only to make them live out his most perverse fantasies — filth and disfigurement — which he says take place in the name of Art and Liberty and always for the first time in his life.)

He is pacing back and forth in the living-room of his apartment thinking about the female character in his piece. He knows he is the man.

'Camille could very well represent this woman,' he says. 'Very beautiful, with a statuesque body. Her face is often like a mask... But Myriam couldn't, no, Myriam is much too blond, too fragile. Myriam would make a better Ophelia with her loosened hair catching in the thorns of the riverbank. A frozen pond landscape. Maybe she could appear dressed in white, with blood flowing from a wound in her forehead. She would kneel down in the middle of the stage with blood on her white tunic. She could also be crying. You would hear her distinctly.'

'So the set is gray and cold. The characters are the woman in red, giving birth, the woman in white, weeping. And the man in royal blue. Music by Prokofieff. A congealed feeling. The cry. Another man, neutral, in black. Turtleneck sweater and corduroy trousers. He's casually smoking a cigarette in the foreground. You see his profile. He is silent. During the whole piece he will be the emotionless witness of the drama. The woman in red lies down on the ground. You hear her breathing heavily. The man leans over the woman's supine body. With his hand on the bulging belly, his gestures express both tenderness and fanaticism toward this body. She convulsively turns her head from side to side. You have the impression she is about to explode.'

He goes to the window and looks out into the street lit by the moon. The telephone rings again, but he knows it's Camille and doesn't answer. He tells himself he mustn't break the creative surge. Something is happening inside him, something essential. This evening he doesn't need Camille — in fact, he will no longer have any need for her or her statuesque body, so perfect in its fluid fullness, since she is there on the ground, swollen and imploring. He thinks about this body that was too recent, too recently in his arms and he tells himself he could love it better once it became a memory, and that he prefers gestures when he reinvents them, and that he has only ever loved anyone cruelly. He stiffens. The ringing has bothered him. He is enraged at Camille's perseverance. He thinks: 'I should burst her, like an abscess.'

He begins pacing the room again, his hands behind his back. He pours himself another drink. He lights a lamp. When he speaks, his voice is stranger, more contained.

'A knife suddenly, in the man's hands,' he says. 'With tender and fanatic gestures he lets the blade caress the beautiful, familiar face — the eyes, forehead, cheeks. Below the chin, the flesh is soft and vulnerable. Lets it run the length of her sides, then traces the legs, the knees, the feet. Lingers on the warm belly, revels in its protrusion. Then, with the tip, very softly, enters at the breach, very softly. The robe is lifted, the thighs open. The shadowy flower revealed. Oh the trickle of poisonous dew! She continues turning her head. There would be a bed at the back of the stage, with Myriam on her knees, her hands gripping the copper bars; you would see her back trembling.'

He sits down. His palms have grown moist. He sees the scene very clearly, these women at his mercy. He is both actor and witness, the man in blue, the man in black. He trembles.

'At this moment, the child should come,' he says. 'The man should cut the cord with the same knife. And there should be lots of blood, the blood should splatter the whole set. The cry,' he says, 'would be a cry of deliverance. The cry would burst forth at the same time as the child is born from the mother, come from the mother and the child at the same time. The night would be final,' he says in a strong voice. 'The curtain would fall on the set thus rendered useless. With the actors gone home, the characters' souls would wander endlessly through the empty room.'

And there, the curtain has fallen on him too. For this man, the curtain always falls too soon. He has never seen the end of the pieces he thinks up. He goes to the telephone which is no longer ringing. He hesitates, and then abruptly turns and leaves, slamming the door. Outside, the street is quiet, only a light wind moves the leaves. He breathes deeply. Nothing but darkness and sleep. The night and the moon, nothing else. A streetlamp feebly lights up the facades.

'A definitive night,' he says again, but without magic, without madness. Maybe if I closed my eyes, and opened them again, I would see the light finally appear. At the heart of a great silence it would furtively slip in to. A sea bird would skim very lightly across the crest of the waves.'

He closes his eyes, and reopens them. The street is the same, empty and quiet. He goes to his car. A violent crash as the door slams shut, the engine roars — the steed rears up and whinnies under the riding crop before throwing itself into a tumultuous gallop. A volubile night after all. He turns on the radio. A Beethoven symphony drowns out the murmurings of the sleeping city. He opens the windows and turns up the sound. He flies, his foot crushing the accelerator. If I could only smash into a tree, he thinks, and everything could finally finish in a burst of metal and broken glass.

For the scenario is always the same for this man. He searches for something which invariably disappears just when he is on the point of reaching it. It's as though he woke up before the dream came to an end, always the same dream. He is searching for something that can't be found. Some have called this thing the Grail, others called it God, still others Eternity. He searches through words. Through literature, his and others'. He searches in orgasm, in the gentleness and the violence of orgasm. He thinks that only fragility can provide him with this lasting element, and that is why he only establishes fleeting contacts with other people. He searches during working hours when he sorts letters at the Ministry of Communications. In the early evening, in the trendy bars, he is still searching. And in the monotonous streets, at night, with a girl on his arm. And in the eyes of his conquests, when their gaze founders, in their sighs and their cries. And also by candlelight, over the remains of a tasty supper, and in the chance beds, and staggering through a pale dawn with stains on his wrinkled scarf.

This evening again, he thought he would find it. He almost did. The images were surging forth, dazzling. He had words at the brink of his lips, he was ready to say them. 'This evening,' he thinks, 'it was the damn phone that broke the spell.' He is angry at Camille, or perhaps Myriam, whichever one is responsible for the failure.

He drives around for some time more, and then, slows down at a busy corner. An inspiration.

'What if I went to the *Bar Carolle*,' he says, 'and scared up some little intellectual, with ideals, a romantic, or a feminist or a mystic, the minute she got those big langorous eyes...'

He parks his car. Checks his hair in the rear-view mirror, arranges his scarf a little more casually around his neck. Gets out. On the sidewalk he lights a cigarette before he disappears into the night.

'Sisyphe' was published in *Moebius* 31 (Winter, 1987).

Thirteen Chrysanthemum Avenue

Thirteen Chrysanthemum Avenue. The house is in a rustic style, pink brick, a grey sloping roof. In front, an impeccably mowed lawn, dense and thick underfoot. Stonework, a few rosebushes, a border of cedars. In the backyard, the patio, a white plastic table with a flowered parasol, a large pool where the deep blue water reflects the cloudless sky. Two weeping willows near the fence. It is the thirteenth hour and the sun darkens.

The noises are those you usually hear in the summer, on a Saturday in the suburbs: lawn mowers, cries of children playing in the pools, a neighbour's radio playing some hit parade between commercials, far away a baby's scream, dogs barking. The smells go with the noises: charcoal-grilled meat, suntan lotion, cut grass.

Thirteen Chrysanthemum Avenue. Upstairs, a dormer window. In the window, the face of an adolescent watching the street, her chin in her hands. She's in her bedroom. Let's call her Anne, like the girl who didn't see anything coming. The sun is calling her: her pink bathing suit is on the bed. Her parents have gone to the market; her little brother is at a kids' party a few streets away. She's alone at the window, facing this street where nothing ever happens. She watches, disenchanted. Her bathing suit is on the bed, next to the black angora cat who is overwhelmed by the heat and occasionally opens big imploring eyes. For two weeks a heat wave has hung over the region. Thirteen Chrysanthemum Avenue, July thirteenth, the thirteenth hour.

She looks at her watch. Thinks: this should be a lucky day, I am thirteen years old, this is the thirteenth of July, the thirteenth hour. What are we waiting for, why isn't luck knocking at my door? She thinks: the telephone could ring, right now, and it would be Julien inviting me to the movies tonight. Julien is the boy she has a crush on. Later, it's thirteen minutes after the thirteenth hour and she thinks: the phone could ring, right now, and I would have won a holiday in a five-star hotel in Japan or the Antilles. I would take Julien along.

Luck seems to have gone somewhere else. Anne turns away from the window and the dismal street. She takes off her nightgown and puts on her bathing suit. Dives into the pool now, into the deep blue water. Later we see her floating in the fresh water, then stretched out on her towel in the grass, sipping a lemonade. Still later, she falls asleep on her stomach, her head on her folded arms. Her parents come home and find her there. During the meal outside she is morose and nibbles at her hamburger. She takes refuge in her room. Night falls. From the dormer window she sees the moon tinted orange and drowning in the mist. She thinks: in a few hours it will be over. It will never again be July thirteenth at thirteen Chrysanthemum Avenue, the year I'm thirteen. So what do I do?

She put on pink lipstick and eyeshadow. Her beach sandals, her old blue jeans, her big light-green T-shirt. The whole family is in the backyard. She goes out without a word. The street welcomes her. Sprinklers are spraying the lawns — the light sound of water projected in a fine drizzle. Farther off, the boulevard. Farther still, she thinks, the city. Hitchhiking on a night like this, what a temptation. She sticks out her thumb; the thirteenth car is sure to stop. She'll say she just wants to get across the bridge. On the other side of the river the lights are dancing. Something will happen; there is a full moon tonight. Anne feels her heart beating wildly.

The thirteenth car, a big dark blue American make, pulls up noiselessly a few meters from her. She runs to the door. I'd like to cross the bridge, she says. The driver nods his head. She slips into the leather seat. A click as the doors lock. From the corner of her eye, she examines the driver's profile. He has bushy eyebrows, a thin moustache on his upper lip, and black hair curling on his neck. The car is air-conditioned. The windows are hermetically-sealed, and music, a cello quartet, invades the space. They pass lines of houses just like her own, with flower-beds edged by cedars and rhododendron. Far away, beyond the bridge the neon lights dance wildly, their colours clash, songs ring out.

Before they get to the bridge they pass by a small woods. Anne thinks : July thirteenth, my thirteenth year, a full moon. What if bad luck were to knock at my door? She watches the driver out of the corner of her eye. There's a swelling between his thighs. What if he were to touch me, she thinks, suddenly chilled. The cellos grate — what gloomy music. She turns her head. The trees at the edge of the road are swaying. I will not see when he undoes his zipper, she thinks, I will not see that thing burst out, or the splatters on the leather seat.

But now they've crossed the bridge that stretches over the dark river and the car pulls up silently at the edge of the road. What's happened to the lights that were dancing so brightly? The street is dark in spite of the streetlamps. I'd like to go farther, she says. The man nods. I'd like to go where there's a party. The car pulls away again smoothly. And I'd like different music. He changes the cassette. A piano sonata. Now he's opened the windows but the city sounds only reach her faintly — it is so hot. On the terraces, waiters with napkins over their arms, are waiting for clients. Everything is in slow motion. The city seems in mourning, she thinks.

They are moving slowly. Later they're in the country, on route thirteen. The weight Anne had in her chest lightens. The man is still just as taciturn. In the glove compartment there is a flask of cognac and a glass. Now and again he pours himself a drink and offers her some. The heat makes its way through her. In the sky, the moon is turning red. Anne turns toward the driver. It's like a ball of fire. Where are we going? she asks. But he doesn't answer. The countryside grows more and more dense. Trees, trees and more trees. The sound of water nearby, probably a river. The wind in the leaves, crackling, screeching. Brutalities concealed by the darkness, owls ready to pounce on careless prey.

The car takes a lane that rises to the left. After a grove of firs and spruces, Anne suddenly sees the large garden with the chrysanthemums, and then the house. A smell of new materials mixed with the perfume of flowers, impregnates the area.

Next to the door is a plaque with the number thirteen engraved on it. The man turns off the engine. Above, a faintly lit dormer window, where she sees the outline of a cat arching its back. Here you are, says the stranger, speaking for the first time. Where? she asks. I don't hear any laughter from the party. It is midnight. Anne gets out of the car. She walks around the house. The pool is right there, with two willows reflected in it. The pink bathing suit hangs over a lawnchair. When she comes back toward the garden, the car has disappeared.

'Jour de chance' from *XYZ* (No.13, 1988).